Dear Parent:

Your child's love of reading starts here!

Every child learns to read in a different way and at his or her own speed. Some go back and forth between reading levels and read favorite books again and again. Others read through each level in order. You can help your young reader improve and become more confident by encouraging his or her own interests and abilities. From books your child reads with you to the first books he or she reads alone, there are I Can Read Books for every stage of reading:

SHARED READING

Basic language, word repetition, and whimsical illustrations, ideal for sharing with your emergent reader

BEGINNING READING

Short sentences, familiar words, and simple concepts for children eager to read on their own

READING WITH HELP

Engaging stories, longer sentences, and language play for developing readers

READING ALONE

Complex plots, challenging vocabulary, and high-interest topics for the independent reader

I Can Read Books have introduced children to the joy of reading since 1957. Featuring award-winning authors and illustrators and a fabulous cast of beloved characters, I Can Read Books set the standard for beginning readers.

A lifetime of discovery begins with the magical words "I Can Read!"

Visit www.icanread.com for information
on enriching your child's reading experience.

Especially for Chloe—enjoy.
—R.S.

I Can Read® and I Can Read Book® are trademarks of HarperCollins Publishers.

Splat the Cat and the Obstacle Course
Copyright © 2021 by Rob Scotton
All rights reserved. Printed in the United States of America.
No part of this book may be used or reproduced in any manner whatsoever without written permission except
in the case of brief quotations embodied in critical articles and reviews. For information address HarperCollins
Children's Books, a division of HarperCollins Publishers, 195 Broadway, New York, NY 10007.
www.icanread.com

Library of Congress Control Number: 2020941019
ISBN 978-0-06-269716-5 (trade bdg.)—ISBN 978-0-06-269715-8 (pbk.)

21 22 23 24 25 LSCC 10 9 8 7 6 5 4 3 2 1 ❖ First Edition

Splat the Cat
and the Obstacle Course

Based on the bestselling books by Rob Scotton
Cover art by Rick Farley
Text by Laura Driscoll
Interior illustrations by Robert Eberz

HARPER
An Imprint of HarperCollins*Publishers*

"Ah," said Splat with a sigh.

He stretched

and looked outside.

It was a sunny summer Saturday—

a day full of possibility.

5

"Splat!" his dad called.
"You are taking your sister
to dance class today.
Remember?"

No! thought Splat.

That was today?

"But Dad," Splat argued,

"Plank made an obstacle course

in his backyard . . ."

But Mom was firm, too.
"Dad and I have to clean out
the garage," she said.
Splat could not argue with that.

So Splat took Flo to dance class.

They had to walk

right by Plank's house.

9

At dance class,

Splat sulked.

What kind of excitement

was he was missing at Plank's?

Here, there was nothing interesting

to see.

On the way home,

Flo spotted the fun at Plank's.

"Ooo!" said Flo. "What's that?"

Flo went in to check out

the obstacle course.

"You're too little!" Splat called after her.

"Maybe you can watch!"

13

Splat looked around.

"Whoa," he said in wonder.

Plank's obstacle course was stunning.

"Yoo-hoo, Splat!" Flo called
from the hanging rings.

Splat gasped.

"Flo! Be careful!"

His little sister was in danger!

And Splat was in charge of her.

"I will save you!" Splat shouted.

Splat started across the rings.

His arms got tired in the middle.

Now Flo was on the bridge.

Splat had to get to her!

"Flo! I am coming!" he cried.

Splat almost slipped off the bridge.

He caught himself—

then made it across upside down.

Meanwhile Flo was halfway

across the stepping stones.

"Slow down, Flo!"

Splat cried.

"You'll trip and fall!"

Just then,

Splat stubbed his toe on a stone.

"Whoa!"

Splat bounced off the trampoline.

Splat flipped over Flo.

Splat landed in the mud.

SPLAT!

"Wow, Splat," said Plank.

"You got the fastest time so far!"

"Well done!" Flo said.

But it was Splat

who was impressed with Flo.

Her strength!

Her balance!

Her speed!

"That's my sister!"

Splat declared proudly.

The next Saturday,

Plank's obstacle course was still open.

"Rematch?" Flo asked Splat.

Splat nodded.

"But first . . . ," Splat said,

"dance class."